ISBN 0-86163-661-9

Text and illustrations copyright © 1995 Sue Hall
This edition copyright © 1995 Award Publications Limited

First published 1995
Second impression1996

Published by Award Publications Limited,
1st Floor, 27 Longford Street,
London NW1 3DZ

Printed in Belgium

Snatch...
... in a mess

by **Sue Hall**

AWARD PUBLICATIONS LIMITED

Snatch looked round him. What a mess! There were toys everywhere and no room left to play with them.

Normally this didn't bother Snatch, he would just step over anything that was in the way. But today it annoyed him because he had just trodden on one of his friends, who seemed quite happy to be making even more of a mess.

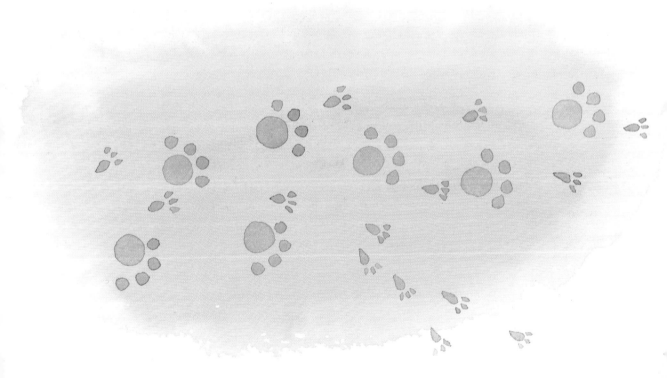

Snatch looked at all his friends. Smutty and Primrose, the cats, had left their toys all over the place for anybody to fall over; and the two bears, Boris and Horace, never, ever, put anything away.

Spencer and Mark, the two mice, had been nibbling at the cheese and had left crumbs all over the tablecloth.

Snatch called all his friends together and told them that they had to help him clean up. They were puzzled by this because they knew that Snatch didn't usually worry about things being in a mess.

But they had to agree with Snatch that things could be tidier and anyway, he was the biggest and cleverest. They knew that because Snatch had told them so. But they mumbled to each other that Snatch was as untidy as all of them put together!

Snatch got a bucket of hot soapy water and his friends found mops and brushes and dusters and they all started cleaning.

It took nearly all day for Snatch and his friends to clean up and put all their toys neatly away.

When it was done they were rather tired; poor Spencer had stopped for a nap halfway through the work. But they felt very pleased with themselves as they looked round at the tidy toys – it did look better. Snatch was right, he did know best.

"We shall be able to find our own things easily, instead of spending hours hunting for them," said Primrose, smiling.

"And we'll have more room to run around without falling over all those toys," said Boris.

Snatch suggested having a tea-party to celebrate, and in all the excitement no one noticed a small box on the floor that was wobbling in a strange way, nor did they hear a faint tapping noise . . . in fact no one had even noticed that Mark Mouse was missing.

Snatch decided that it was up to him to sort out the monster. After all, he knew he was the biggest and cleverest. But he wasn't very brave. "Oh dear," he thought, "I wish now that I was the smallest." Snatch went slowly up to the box, which had stopped moving by now. A tiny little squeak came from inside it.

Snatch pushed the box with his nose and, to everyone's amazement, out popped Mark Mouse, looking very sad. "Please don't tidy me up again," he cried. "Nobody even noticed that I wasn't at the tea-party."

"Never mind, Mark, there is plenty left for you. Come and sit down," they all shouted together.

It was a lovely party and they were so pleased that there hadn't been a monster in the box after all.

After tea they played with all their toys. But when they stopped and looked round, they saw more of a mess then there had been before!

"Never mind," sighed Snatch. "It's probably better this way. At least we are used to being in a mess," And he went off to his basket.

As Snatch settled down to sleep, he thought about what a busy day it had been with all that tidying up and all that making a mess again. But at least Mark Mouse was safe, and there were no monsters in boxes. He was happy.

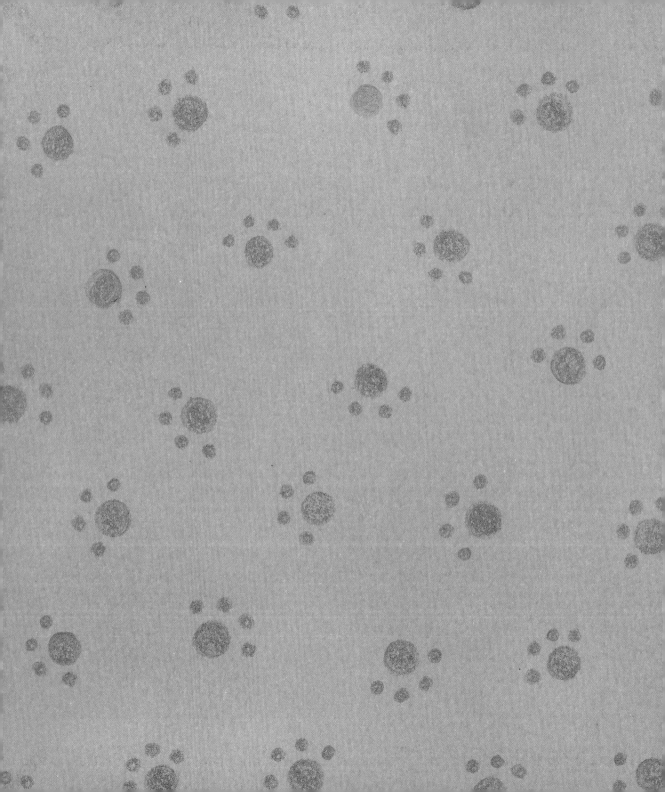